P9-BYG-895

I Never Knew Your Name

I Never Knew Your Name

by Sherry Garland *illustrated by* Sheldon Greenberg

Ticknor & Fields Books for Young Readers

New York 1994

Published by Ticknor & Fields Books for Young Readers
A Houghton Mifflin company, 215 Park Avenue South,
New York, New York 10003

Manufactured in the United States of America

Book design by David Saylor
The text of this book is set in 15 point Galliard Bold
The illustrations are oil paintings reproduced in full color

HOR 10 9 8 7 6 5 4 3 2 1

LIBRARY OF CONGRESS CATALOGING-IN-PUBLICATION DATA
Garland, Sherry.
I never knew your name / by Sherry Garland ; illustrated
by Sheldon Greenberg. p. cm.
Summary: A small boy laments the lonely life of a teenage
suicide whose neighbors didn't even know his name.
ISBN 0-395-69686-0
[1. Suicide—Fiction. 2. Friendship—Fiction.]
I. Greenberg, Sheldon, ill. II Title.
PZ7.G18415Iam 1994
[Fic]—dc20 93-23703 CIP AC

For John F.—hold on to your dreams

Sherry Garland

For Lee Ann

Sheldon Greenberg

I never knew your name
and you didn't know mine,
but I'm the kid
who moved in across the street
not long ago.

The first time I saw you,
you were shooting hoops in the moonlight.
It was way past midnight
but I was still awake,
waiting for my father to visit.
He never did show up.

It was cool the way the basketball
would disappear into the shadows.
I heard the bounce,
then a swish—
over and over.
Man, you were good.

I never saw you play
with the other guys from the corner;
Too bad for them—
you were really good.

You liked to feed the stray dog
that hung around our block.
I heard your mom yell at you
that day you brought it home,
but you snuck it in anyway, sometimes,
until the landlord called the city pound,
and they took it away.

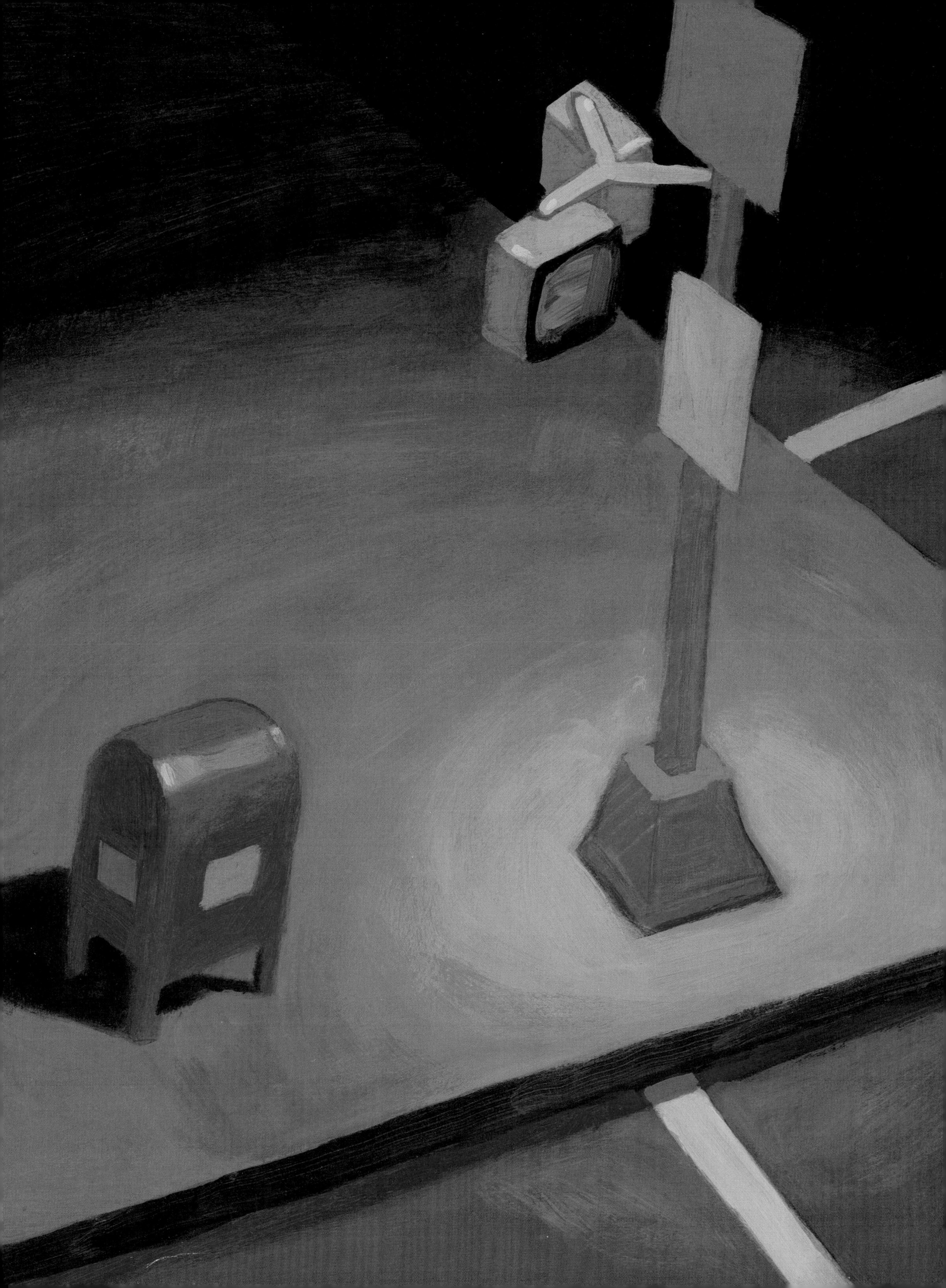

Anyone could see you had a crush on my big sister—
the way you watched her when she walked by,
giggling with her friends,
acting like she could care less.
I don't think she meant to call you names
and make fun of your clothes.
I guess that's the way big sisters are.

I saw you sitting on the curb
throwing gravel at the lamppost
the night the other guys went to the prom,
all dressed up in fancy suits
with white carnations.

Me, I'd rather go fishing,
and I would have, too,
if my dad had visited like he promised.

I almost climbed out my window that night
with my rod and reel,
to ask if you wanted to go down to the pond
on the other side of the park.
There probably weren't any fish in it anyway.

So I didn't say a thing
and went to sleep to the sound of pebbles
clanging against the lamppost.

That last day,
you were up on the roof
feeding the pigeons.
I grabbed a handful of bread
and started to go up there, too,
but you looked like you were crying
and wanted to be alone,
so I went and watched
a boring old movie on TV instead.

That night, the ambulance screaming under my window woke me up and made the dogs howl.

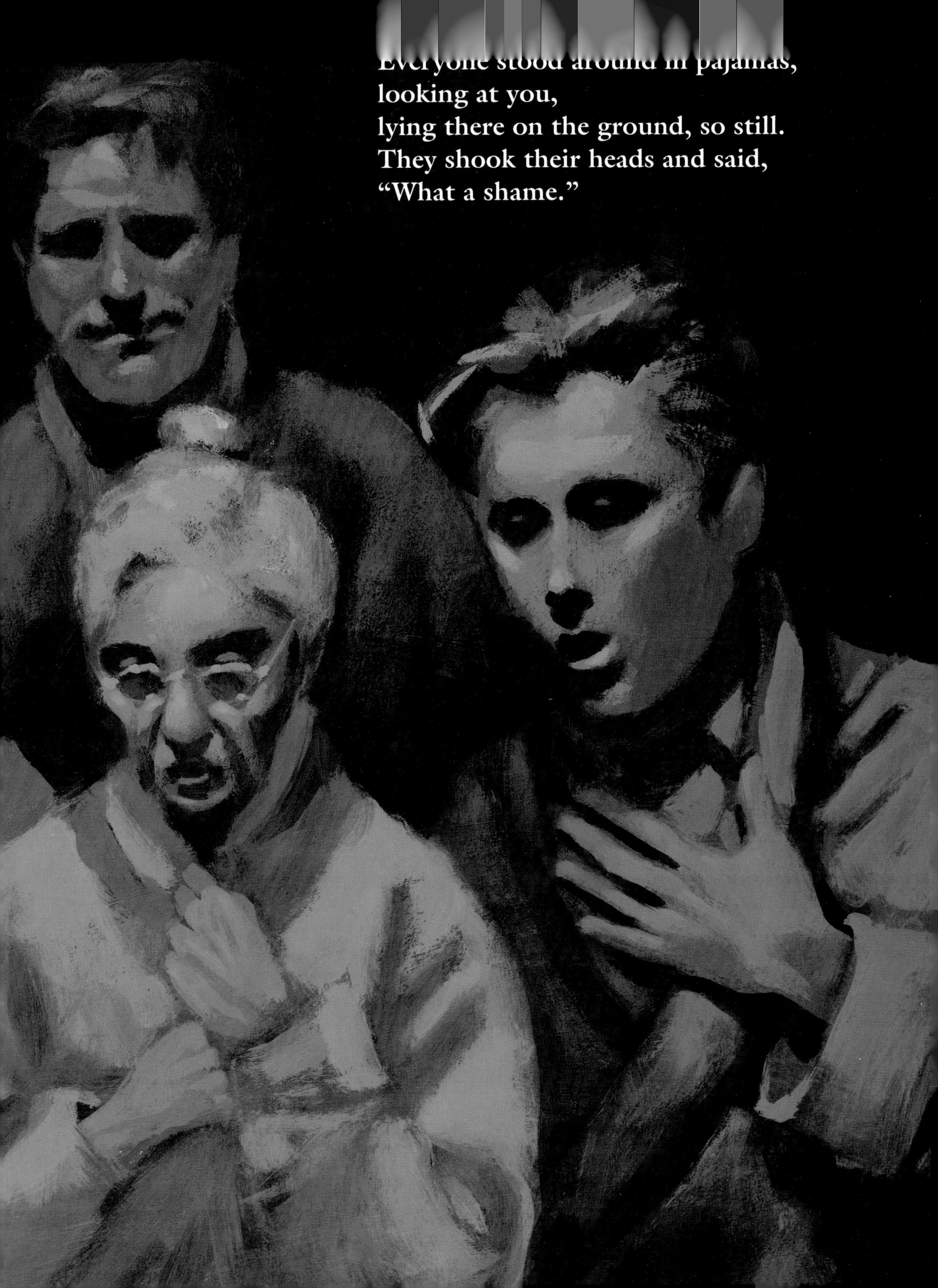

Everyone stood around in pajamas,
looking at you,
lying there on the ground, so still.
They shook their heads and said,
"What a shame."

I saw your picture on the news.
It was just like the one in the yearbook
my sister left on the kitchen table,
after the police cars had gone
and the apartments were quiet again.

She said you weren't so bad
and she didn't know why you did it.

Next morning on the way to school,
everyone was talking about you,
even though most of the kids
couldn't remember who you were.
I told the older guys
you sure could shoot hoops.

After school I climbed up on the roof
and fed the pigeons.
I told them you wouldn't be coming anymore.
Then I scratched your name
in the concrete ledge.

I'm sorry I never knew your name.
I wish we could have been friends.